The Chocolate-Covered-Cookie TANTRUM

by Deborah Blumenthal ★ Pictures by Harvey Stevenson

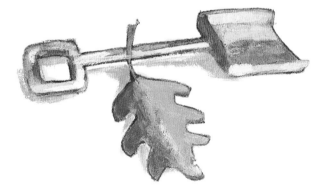

CLARION BOOKS/New York

Clarion Books
a Houghton Mifflin Company imprint
3 Park Avenue, 19th Floor, New York, New York 10016
Text copyright © 1996 by Deborah Blumenthal
Illustrations copyright © 1996 by Harvey Stevenson

The illustrations for this book were executed in acrylics.
The text is set in 18/21-point Amasis medium.

For information about permission to reproduce selections from
this book, write to trade.permissions@hmheo.com or to
Permissions, Houghton Mifflin Harcourt Publishing Company,
3 Park Avenue, 19th Floor, New York, New York 10016.

Manufactured in China.

Library of Congress Cataloging-in-Publication Data

Blumenthal, Deborah.
    The chocolate-covered-cookie tantrum / by Deborah
Blumenthal ; pictures by Harvey Stevenson.
        p.   cm.
        Summary: Seized with a desire for a cookie
while in the park, Sophie discovers that throwing a terrible
tantrum will not get her what she wants.
        ISBN 0-395-68699-7   PA ISBN 0-395-70028-0
        [1. Temper tantrums—Fiction. 2. Behavior—
        Fiction.]
    1. Stevenson, Harvey, ill.   II. Title.
PZ7.B6267Ch   1997
[E]—dc20 95-21083
CIP
AC

SCP 25 24 23 22 21 20
4500689782

To Sophie
—D.B.

For Jack
—H.S.

Late one afternoon
on the way home from the park

Sophie saw a girl eating
a chocolate-covered cookie.
It looked delicious.
Sophie wanted one too.

"I want a cookie," said Sophie.
"I want *that* cookie."

"I'm sorry," said her mother.
"I don't have any cookies now,
and it's almost time for supper."

But Sophie didn't care about supper.
She wanted a chocolate-covered cookie.

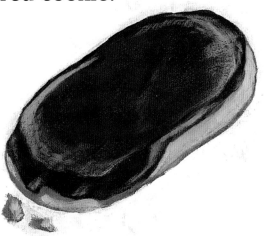

"I want one,"
Sophie yelled.
"I WANT ONE!"

"I know you do,"
said her mother.
"But I don't have one."

"**GET ONE!**" yelled Sophie, shaking her arms and legs and dropping to the ground.

"**I WANT ONE!**" she yelled, shaking her head from side to side, banging her feet on the ground.

"**I WANT A COOKIE! I WANT A COOKIE!**"

"Sophie," said her mother, "let's go home and then we'll see about cookies."

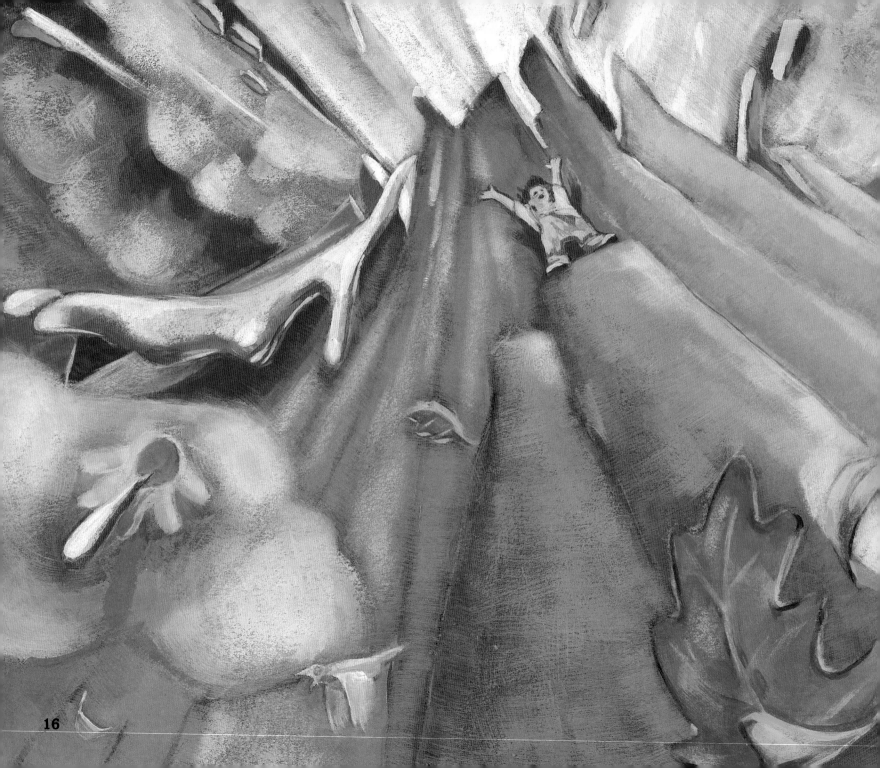

But Sophie didn't want to go home.
She didn't want supper.

She just wanted the cookie.
THE COOKIE!
THE COOKIE!

She cried and cried and cried to get the cookie.
She cried so much her face felt hot as a pepper.
She was so mad she couldn't stop.
She kicked her legs into the air
and pounded her heels into the ground.
She kicked and pounded
and kicked and pounded
and kicked
and kicked
and kicked
and kicked
and kicked.

She rubbed her sneakers into the sidewalk
and rolled her head back and forth
and rocked it up and down.

"Sophie," her mother asked,
"do you want to finish your banana?"

Noooooooooooooooooooooooooooooooooo!" said Sophie.
"**NO BANANA, NO BANANA, NOBANANA!**"
She didn't want banana.
She just wanted the cookie.
THE COOKIE!
THE COOKIE!

Sophie cried
and cried
and cried
and cried
until
the trees
and the ground
and the sky
started to rumble
and tumble
and spin
and turn

and
go
around
and
around
and
around
and AROUND

until
everything
stopped.

Then
she took in a big shaky breath
and got up.

"I want my blanket," said Sophie.
"Here," said her mother.
Sophie pulled it to her face.

"Now we'll go," said her mother.
"Umm," said Sophie.

She took her mother's hand,
and they walked home.

On the couch,
she fell asleep.

And when she woke up,
she ate all her supper
until there was nothing left.

Then her mother surprised her.
She put a chocolate-covered cookie
on her plate.

Sophie took a big bite.
A smile spread over her face.

"I *like* cookies," said Sophie.

"Yes," said her mother.
"I know you do."